1 9 9 2

Unravelling Words & the Weaving of Water

Cecilia Vicuña

TRANSLATED BY ELIOT WEINBERGER
AND SUZANNE JILL LEVINE

EDITED AND INTRODUCED
BY ELIOT WEINBERGER

GRAYWOLF PRESS

Publication of this volume is made possible in part by a grant provided by the
Minnesota State Arts Board, through an appropriation by the Minnesota State
Legislature, and by a grant from the National Endowment for the Arts. Addi-
tional support has been provided by the Jerome Foundation, the Northwest Area
Foundation, and other generous contributions from foundations, corporations,
and individuals. Graywolf Press is a member agency of United Arts, Saint Paul.

Published by Graywolf Press, 2402 University Avenue, Suite 203,
Saint Paul, Minnesota 55114. All rights reserved.

9 8 7 6 5 4 3 2
First Printing, 1992

Library of Congress Cataloging-in-Publication Data
Vicuña, Cecilia.
    Unravelling words and the weaving of water / Cecilia Vicuña ; translated
by Eliot Weinberger and Suzanne Jill Levine; edited by Eliot Weinberger.
        p.   cm.
    Text in English and Spanish.
    ISBN 1-55597-166-0 (paper) : $12.00
    I. Weinberger, Eliot.   II. Title.
PQ8098.32.I35A28   1992
861 – dc20   91-44630

Contents

Introduction

"Everything 'dead' trembles,"
writes Wassily Kandinsky in
1913: "Not only the stars, moon, wood, and flowers of which
the poets sing, but also a cigarette butt lying in an ashtray, a
patient white trouser button looking up from a puddle in the
street . . . everything shows me its face, its innermost being,
its secret soul."

At the same moment, the other K of the Rus-
sian avant-garde, Velimir Khlebnikov is writing: "The only
freedom we demand is freedom from the dead."

The Modern-
ist project of exhalting the new and obliterating the rest, of
replacing sunflowers with spark plugs as inspirational source
and imaginative subject, aged faster than the gadgets of its af-
fection. But the opposite drift of the modern – the recovery of
everything, the inclusion of all that had been excluded –
remains vivid, for the continuing lesson of the century is the
sameness of the stuff of the world:

Trouser buttons may have
turned to zippers, but both, like stars and wood, became recognized as merely varying configurations of the same sub-
atomic particles. People were discovered to have the same
dreams, tell the same stories, construct variants of the same
societies. The same genetic rules were applied to clams and
conquerors.

In this brotherhood (sisterhood) of the same,
everything takes on an equal weight: Lautréamont's umbrella
and sewing machine meet (make love) on the dissecting table.
And what they produce – say, a trouser button – becomes as
worthy an object of contemplation as an Alpine sunrise or the
ruins of Karnak.

There's a story that George Washington
Carver had a dream. God appeared before Carver and told him

to ask anything he wanted to know. Carver said, "Tell me everything about the peanut." And God replied: "Your mind is too small to understand a peanut."

And in a world where circular or linear time had been replaced by exploding, simultaneous, Einstein time, what was ancient was the latest news. And the latest news was what the ancients knew all along.

The Modernist enthusiasm for archaic art was not merely a developing taste for simple forms and complex assemblages, as the current history runs. What the Moderns saw were manifestations of power. These strange or common objects were made to control life and death, sex and weather and food and illness. They were meant to change their world.

In the universe of identical things – theirs and now ours – what is not the same, what remains in a state of continual change, is the relation among the things. The same particles spin into hawk and mouse, Anthony and Cleopatra, paint and canvas, Abbott and Costello: the world begins when they collide.

But more: switch them around and it's a different world: mouse and canvas, Abbott and Cleopatra . . .

(Or Cleopatra and her nose. Pascal ruminates: If it had been longer, the face of the world would have changed.)

In the luminous net of relations, the slightest change – even watching – changes it all. Cut a single fern frond and stick it in the middle of a trail. The gesture, nearly everywhere, would be meaningless. In New Guinea, among the Kaluli, it means that the souls of the bananas will not escape from a newly planted field: there'll be food in the months ahead.

Magic is dependent on the power latent in the least conspicuous object. A few fingernail parings can kill a man; a feather can ward off a hurricane. It is the context, and the act of placing in the context, that gives the useless scrap its power.

And what happens when that act occurs outside of its culture – or more exactly, occurs in a culture that does not automatically recognize its significance? What happens, in other words, when Schwitters picks a bus ticket out of a Berlin gutter and pastes it on a canvas alongside similar debris?

As an act of magic, it belongs to a private superstition: a lucky charm in someone else's pocket. And yet a Schwitters bus ticket is strangely numinous: that representation of a world by its most insignifcant member remains far more moving than the contemporary celebrations of dirigibles and hydroelectric plants.

It is a Chinese wisdom: the grass bends under the conquering armies; when they have swept by, it stands up again. The particular is epic.

For twenty years, Cecilia Vicuña has been engaged in similarly useless, significant gestures.

She makes a circle of colored powder on a Pacific beach. She spills a glass of milk on a street in Bogotá. She hides bundles of twigs among the rocks in the hills overlooking that city. She floats tiny rafts in the Hudson. She places clay snakes around a fire hydrant. She ties strings between the boulders near a Peruvian lake. She assembles bits of natural and artificial debris into tiny sculptures she calls *precarios* (precarious things) or *basuritas* (bits of garbage, a little litter).

Descended from the practices of Andean shamans, these are the ritual acts of a personal religion. Their lifespan is negligible, though some linger in individual memories, and a few have been recorded on film. They are the haiku that are written on paper boats to be set out in the lake, the new year's wishes that are burned at midnight.

The objects employed in these rituals are garbage. Not the garbage produced by tribal religion: the works made for a single use, then tossed aside to be collected and exhibited in museums of primitive art. Nor are they trash-heap archives – the midden kingdom – by which we know so many buried cultures. These ritual objects do not become – they are made of – garbage.

But it is nature's garbage, not ours: feathers, shells, driftwood, pebbles, leaves. Pieces of a landscape of debris that came into existence when its normal use was abandoned: when we stopped burning firewood, when we invented new adornments to replace the feathered capes and necklaces of shells.

Tiny bits of nature rescued for a moment: "precarious," Vicuña writes, comes from the Latin *precis*, meaning "prayer."

We may take these sculptures and the acts that created them in the Western sense: brief personal supplications sent to the heavens. Or we may take them as numerous cultures understand prayer: sent from the heavens to earth. A momentary incarnation of the gods in language, or – and Christianity retains this in its cults of "speaking in tongues" – a direct message from them.

What do these gods say? Vicuña gives us, literally, a "clue": a ball of thread. (That which led Theseus out of the labyrinth was transformed with usage into anything that might lead to the solution of a mystery.)

Everywhere in Vicuña's work there are threads and cloth, themselves products of natural debris: the dead hair of animals, the fluff that sends the cotton seeds airborne so that the plant may propagate.

Thread, universally, is what ties people to the gods; its arrangement into warp and woof, cloth and the act of weaving, remains a perennial metaphor for both the complexities and the seamlessness of the world.

And it, too, is prayer: Vicuña points out that both *sutra* and *tantra* mean "thread." It too is language: the Inkas (and possibly the archaic Chinese) wrote in a system of knotted threads suspended from a small stick. The woven and embroidered cloth of countless cultures are historical records, collections of myths, maps of the universe.

For millennia the Andean peoples were unquestionably the most advanced weavers on earth: more than anywhere else, the fabric of their culture is inextricable from fabric itself. What's left of much of it is a few scraps: some of the technical processes are now inimitable; most of the iconographic meaning has dropped out.

These are symbolically the scraps Vicuña drapes over her tiny sticks; the scraps to which she attaches her bits of feather and shell. They are the few pieces of bone from which dinosaurs are reconstructed, the shard that is irrefutable evidence.

Threads and scraps of cloth and scattered remains of natural rubbish: trembling messages from dead cultures and dying nature. Like irregular electromagnetic wave patterns from a distant star, they cannot be decoded, they are anomalies for which our explanations are insufficient. They put us on alert: there may be more going on than we thought.

Her name, which is not a pseudonym, is her totemic animal. Given a word, she unravels the threads of its fabric. Given a twig, a pebble, and a place to stand, she tries to move the earth. She chants to the factories to leave the river be.

The translations in this book were all written in close collaboration – usually in the same room – with the author. This meant that the poems, quite often, took on a life of their own in English that did not replicate a strictly "literal" reading of the original. The texts marked [SJL] were translated by Suzanne Jill Levine with Cecilia Vicuña; those marked [SJL/EW] were written by the three of us; the rest are my collaborations. Vicuña is, above all, an oral poet; for the poems here, the English versions were made thinking first of their performance.

ELIOT WEINBERGER

I

Precarious

And if I devoted my life
to one of its feathers
to living its nature
being it understanding it
until the end

Reaching a time
in which my acts
are the thousand
tiny ribs of the feather
and my silence
the humming the whispering
of wind in the feather
and my thoughts
quick sharp precise
as the non-thoughts
of the feather.

Entering

I thought that all this was perhaps nothing more than a way of remembering.

To remember (*recordar*) in the sense of playing the strings (*cuerdas*) of emotion.

Re-member, *re-cordar*, from *cor, corazón*, heart.

*

First there was listening with the fingers, a sensory memory:
    the shared
bones, sticks and feathers were sacred things I had to arrange.

To follow their wishes was to rediscover a way of thinking: the paths of mind I traveled, listening to matter, took me to an ancient silence waiting to be heard.

To think is to follow the music, the sensations of the elements.

And so began a communion with the sky and the sea, the need to respond to their desires with works that were prayers.

Pleasure is prayer.

If, at the beginning of time, poetry was an act of communion, a form of collectively entering a vision, now it is a space one enters, a spatial metaphor.

*

Metaphor stakes out a space of its own creation.

If the poem is temporal, an oral temple, form is a spatial temple.

Metapherein: to carry beyond
                    to the other contemplation:
to con-temple the interior and the exterior.

Space and time, two forms of motion that cross for a moment,
        an instant
                    of doubled pleasure, concentration, con-
penetration.

                              *

The precarious is that which is obtained through prayer.

To pray is to feel.

"The quipu that remembers nothing," an empty string, was
my first precarious work.

I prayed by making a quipu, offering the desire to remember.

Desire is the offering, the body is nothing but a metaphor.

                              *

In ancient Peru the diviner would trace lines of dust in the
earth, as a means of divination, or of letting the divine speak
through him.

Lempad, in Bali, says: "All art is transient, even stone wears
away." "God tastes the essence of the offerings, and the
people eat the material remains."

                              *

To recover memory is to recover unity:

                To be one with sea and sky
                To feel the earth as one's own skin
                Is the only kind of relationship
                That brings her joy.

                              (*New York, 1983–1991*)

Five Notebooks for Exit Art

I.

CONNECTION

The art of joining, union
from *ned:* to bind, to tie
zero grade form: *nod*
old English: *net*
Latin: *nodus*
knot

David Brower said: "The earth is dying because people don't see the connections" between a hamburger and the death of the rain forest, air conditioning and the death of the atmosphere).

Eliot Weinberger said: "Do you know what a *clue* is? A ball of yarn or thread that Theseus used to come out of the labyrinth, thus anything that guides or directs in the solution of a problem."

René Guénon says: "the connection protects."

in Nahuatl, one of the names of God is "nearness and togetherness" (. . . *del cerca y del junto*)

II.

The Resurrection of the Grasses

Octavio Paz said: "Poetry is resurrection."

> to be erect
> again,
> greening!

> waves
> of
> grass

> blades
> blades

> surging
> from the
> dead streams

> resurrect!
> *surgere*
> *sub + regere:*
> to lead

> lead the
> greening
> upright!

growth, green & grass
originally had the same root:
> *ghre*

once I dreamt of a form of poetry created by
the sound of feet walking in the grass

in Nahuatl, poetry, *xopancuicatl* is "a cele-
bration of life and cyclical time: the poem and
the poet become a plant that grows with the
poem; the plant becomes the fibers of the
book in which the poem is painted . . ."
(Eliot Weinberger)

collected all
around waterways
in Brooklyn,
Manhattan, Chile
and the Bronx,

the land grasses
and the
cochayuyo
seaweed

are intertwined
with plastic
nets.

resurrect!

III.

The Origin of Weaving

origin
from *oriri:* the coming out of the stars

weave
from *weban, wefta,* Old English
weft, cross thread
web

> the coming out
> of the cross-star
>
> the interlacing of
> warp and weft

to imagine the first cross
intertwining of branches and twigs
to make a nest
to give birth

the first spinning of a thread
to cross spiraling
a vegetable fiber imitating a vine

the first thread coming out of fleece trapped in
vegetation

the first cross of warp and weft
union of high and low, sky and earth,
woman and man

the first knot, beginning of the spiral:
life and death, birth and rebirth

textile, text, context
from *teks:* to weave, to fabricate, to make wicker or
                wattle for mud-covered walls (Paternosto)

sutra: sacred Buddhist text
                thread (Sanskrit)

tantra: sacred text derived from the Vedas: thread

ching: as in *Tao Te Ching* or *I Ching*
                sacred book: warp
                wei: its commentaries: weft

Quechua: the sacred language
                derived from *q'eswa:*
                rope or cord made of straw

to weave a new form of thought:
                connect
bring together in one

IV.

PUEBLO DE ALTARES

pueblo: people
altar: "place for burning sacrificial offerings"

> we are the pueblo
> our house the altar

threshold: limit or doorway

lintel, the top of the threshold
from *liminaris,* the limit
and the most ancient *tol:* as in *dolmen:*
table of stone

> *mesa* & *missa*
> (the mass, from "sending a message")
> are also confused

(*limit* and *lumen:*
the light came to be one)

to confuse is "to pour together"

house & altar are intertwined
as in architecture
from *arch*
> *arkhe,* rule, beginning
> or *ar,* to fit together as in bow & arrow
> & *tektron:* carpenter, builder, from
> *teks:* to weave

"to make wicker or wattle fabric for mud-covered
houses"

coming from the beach, the little residues reside in it

Patti Hagan says "they look like the scale model of a lost civilization."

someone else said: "or a new civilization built on the remains of the present one."

in Panama, the people made homeless by the U.S. bombing were called *precaristas*

favelas, callampas, pueblos jovenes, villas miserias, shan-tytowns by any name are all
                    Pueblos de altares

V.

PONCHO: RITUAL DRESS

hilo de agua
thread of water

hilo de vida
thread of life

they say woolly animals
are born high in the
mountain springs

water and fiber
are one

wool & cotton
downy fiber
an open hand

the Cotton Mother textile gooddess in Chavín is a plant crea-
ture with snake feet, eyes and heart radiating from the center
like a sun

the poncho
is a book
a woven
message

a metaphor
spun

white stones found in the mist, the *illa* and the *enqaychu* are
the emblems of the vital force within the woolly animals themselves but only the poor and haggard can find them by the
springs.

[written in English]

13

Ten Metaphors in Space

CON CÓN

At the junction of the two waters, the Aconcagua River and the
Pacific Ocean, I made my first spiral.

(*Con Cón, Chile, 1966*)

Autumn

In June 1971 I filled the Forestal Gallery of the National Museum of Fine Arts in Santiago, Chile, with leaves. The work was dedicated to the construction of socialism and lasted three days.

Antivero

The river wants to be heard before it is contaminated.

The *ñipas* are its spirits, its guardians. The perfumed shrub.

Thread is a trail

      I'm lost on

the trail is a scent

      I travel

The Chibcha Trail

The Chibchas wove trails on the crests of the hills to join the villages of Cundinamarca and Boyacá.

> Poetry lives in certain places
> where the cliffs need nothing
> but a sign to come alive:
> two or three lines, a marking,
> and silence begins to speak.

(Bogotá, 1981)

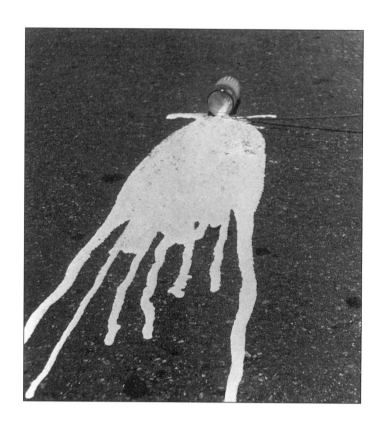

A GLASS OF MILK

In 1979 in Colombia there was a "milk crime": distributors had added powder and water to the milk. 1,920 children died from drinking the contaminated milk.

I announced the spilling of a glass of milk under the blue sky. On the scheduled day I spilled the milk and wrote on the pavement:

> The cow is being
> is the continent spilled
> whose milk What are we doing
> (blood) to our lives?

SIDEWALK FORESTS

Small altars on the streets of New York, air vents for the earth, pasture born in the gutters.

(New York, 1981)

K'IJLLU

Red dust in the k'ijllu crack.

The rock recalls a people that buried its dead with red ocher powder.

The earth leaked red ocher, and a civilization six thousand years old was discovered. *(Salter's Island, Maine, 1985)*

FOR THE TREES AND BIRDS

The opinions of birds are very important. Would they accept these woven trees? In a few minutes they were singing like crazy.

(*Lexington, New York, 1987*)

FIRE HYDRANT

Mouth of water. A little dust and four clay snakes mark the way back to the sea.

(New York, 1990)

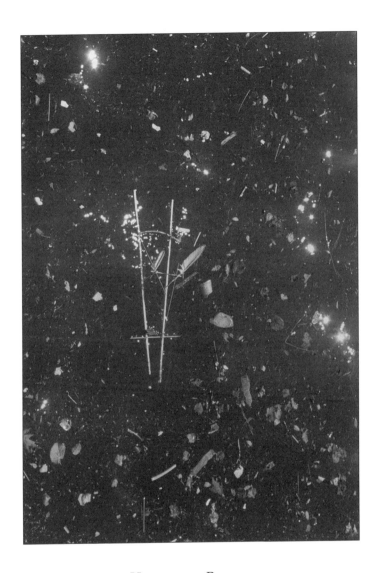

HUDSON RIVER

I launched boats on the river, talking to it. Changing signs, mine and those there by chance. The boats and the trash, mingling.

(*New York, 1990*)

II

Palabrarmás

Open your mouth and receive the host of the wounded word
VICENTE HUIDOBRO

The original book *Palabrarmás* was born from a vision in which individual words opened to reveal their inner associations, allowing ancient and newborn metaphors to come to light.

In 1966 nearly a hundred of these words appeared. I called them *divinations,* and ceased to think much about them.

Then in 1974, they appeared again, arming themselves with a name, *palabrarmás* (*palabra,* word; *labrar,* to work; *armas,* arms; *mas*́, more). A word that means: to work words as one works the land is to work more; to think of what the work does is to arm yourself with the vision of words. And more: words are weapons, perhaps the only acceptable weapons. That same year I began to find ancient and modern texts which helped me to understand what I had seen.

Primero vi una palabra en el aire
sólida y suspendida
mostrándome
su cuerpo de semilla

Se abría y deschacía
y de sus partes brotaban
asociaciones dormidas
                    Enamorados
                            en amor, morado
                            enajenados

Encantándome se sucedían
domos y cúpulas de encanto
cantaban en mí

Ascendía en el vértigo
desbarrancándome
en el quiebre
entre canto y dome
canto y en

Entraba y salía
por palacios desiertos
viendo la imagen
del canto y el entrar
el principio y el final.

La imagen tiene muslos
en su fractal
caderas y llagas
por donde entrar

Ella es madre y ventolera
su cuerpo fino
acomete y espera

I saw a word in the air
solid and suspended
showing me
her seed body

She opened up and fell apart
and from her parts sprouted
sleeping thoughts
                    of love, livid
                                in love, living
                                out of love
came madder violet

Enchanting me
nipples and cupolas
chanting in me

She ascends in a spiral
as I fall in the break
between chant and cupola

In and out
of deserted palaces I wander
seeing the image of chanting
and entering
the beginning
                    the end
                                the word

The fractal image has thighs,
hips and wounds
to enter

She is mother and wind
her lean body
stalks and waits

Busca y atiende
la puerta
con silbante solicitud
la urge amándola
y al golpe terso
del portal
entra rodando
a su lugar

Nadie vería el mismo palacio
una vez cruzado el portal
nadie observaría las mismas flores
más que por un don
de ubicuidad

La coincidencia es un alcance
milagroso del azar
el cruce de dos vectores
poco cuidadosos quizás

Cada palabra
aguarda al viajero
que en ella
espera hallar
senderos y soles
del pensar

Esperan silentes
y cantarinas
cien veces tocadas
y trastocadas
agotadas por un instante
y vueltas a despertar

She seeks
the door
whistling in love
pushing it
with a terse blow as
the door rolls
                in place

No one will see the same palace
once the threshold has been crossed
no one will see the same flowers
except through the gift
of ubiquity

Coincidence is a miracle
of chance, the crossing
of two vectors,
carelessly placed perhaps

Each word
awaits the traveler
hoping to find
in her
trails and suns
of thought

They wait
singing in silence
one hundred times touched
and changed
exhausted for a moment
and then revived

Perdidas o abandonadas
esplenden de nuevez

Cuerpos celestes
cada una
en su movimiento

Estructura cuárzica
al oído y al tacto
interior

Música corporal
sus formas transforman
nacen y mueren
y se solazan
en la unión

Espacio
al que
compenetramos

Amos del com
pene y entrar

Amos y dueños
del palabrar
o aman ellas
nuestro labrar

Lo desean
como nosotros
a ellas.

Lost or abandoned
they shine again

Celestial bodies
each
in its orbit

Quartz structure
sensed by touch
and the inner ear

Body music
forms transform
born to die
enjoying
their conjugation

Space
that we penetrate

Lords of pen
in trance

Lords of words
or do they
love our works?

Do they
desire us as we
desire them?

[SJL]

*

To approach words from poetry is a form of asking questions

To ask questions is to fathom, to drop a hook to the bottom of the sea.

The first questions appeared as a vision: I saw in the air words that contained, at the same time, both a question and an answer.

I called them "divinations." And the words said: the word *is* the divination; to divine is to ascertain the divine.

Other numerical and calendrical systems speak of what has come or what will come, but only the word is the divination of what we are now and why.

In Spanish, *preguntar*, to ask, from the Latin *percontari*, from *contus*, hook.

The insistence on *seeing* words, in their double sense, interior and exterior, is universal. (To write and to read are also ways of seeing.)

"I don't see with my eyes: words
are my eyes"

OCTAVIO PAZ, *A Draft of Shadows*

In Nahuatl, the ancient language of Central Mexico, the sage was called *tlamatini*, "the one who knows something."

> "Those who see
> who dedicate themselves to observing
> the course and ordered ways of heaven
> how is night divided."
>
> *Libro de los coloquios*

To see, from the Indo-European root *wid*, Germanic *wit*, Old English wise, wit, knowledge. Latin *videre*, view, vision. Suffixed form *wid-es-ya*, in Greek *idea*, appearance, form. In Sanskrit *veda*, knowledge and "I have seen."

To divine, from the Indo-European root *da*, *dai* in Greek *daiesthai*, to divide. Suffixed form *dai-mon*, divider, provider, divinity.

A word is divine: internally divided.
Its inner division creates its ambiguity, the inner tension that makes growth and association possible. Division that can be expressed in multiple ways: – putting two parts together, as in root + suffix. – com-pounding, putting two words into one. – putting two antithetical meanings in one.

In Spanish, *ambiguous* is "that which is discussed," divided.

35

Words want to speak; to listen to them is the first task.

To open words is to open oneself.

To discover the ancient metaphors condensed in the word itself.

A history of words would be a history of being, but this writing is only a meditation through hints and fragments – from the imagination, for the imagination.

IMAGEN EN ACCIÓN   image in action

Abrir, to open, in Spanish, from the Latin *aperire*, from *parere*, to give birth, to separate in two parts as in opening a clam shell.

"Name; the word seems to be a compressed sentence, signifying being for which there is a search."

PLATO, *Cratylus*

"The whole delicate substance of speech is built upon substrate of metaphor. Abstract terms, pressed by etymology, reveal their ancient roots still embedded in direct action."

ERNEST FENOLLOSA, *The Chinese Written Character as a Medium for Poetry*

"The first imposers of names were philosophers."

PLATO, *Cratylus*

37

Words take us, mark us, they contain within the ideas that keep us moving.

Every people is its language, the vision they inherit. To create is to set out from the first images, the original pattern.

But throughout history words have concealed and revealed, constantly transforming.

Having lost the memory of the original meaning, we can invent an *etymon* (true meaning), one that contains within what the word will be. To go backward and inward simultaneously. To contemplate the origins and the future. The ancient and current signified.

REVELAR	to reveal
VOLVER A VELAR	to re-veil
CONSIDERAR EL ORIGEN	To consider the origin
ES CON Y SIDERALMENTE	is to con(template)side(really)
CONTEMPLAR EL *oriri:*	study together the *oriri:*
SALIR DE LOS ASTROS:	the coming out of the stars

To enter words in order to see, is the point of word-working: to work speech, to speak watching speech work.

To split the word *word* – and *metaphor* and *poetry:*

"Being inclines intrinsically to self concealment."

HERACLITUS, *Fragment 123*

"In the didactic texts, the Vedic glossaries, the commentaries to the sacred works, still another resource of language is employed. It is the *nirukta,* 'explication of words,' . . . *nirukta* does not presume to be a scientific 'etymology'.

" . . . the explication of *saman,* 'liturgical chant,' from *sa* (she) + *ama* (he), developed at length in the *Chandogya Upanishad,* reminds the poet that by chanting he activates within himself a marriage between two forces, male and female; and elsewhere, the same text gives for the same word, a totally different explanation . . . This digression seemed necessary to underline the *spiritually practical* (and not intellectually discursive) value of the Hindu verbal elaborations."

RENÉ DAUMAL, *Rasa*

Palabra [word], from the Latin
parabola, resemblance, from the
Greek *parabole,* from *paraballo:*
to put beside.

The word *compares* puts side by side what is known and
what is to be known.

To work words is to be with, to con-verse – what the
word says about being is what we will know.

C O N O C E R	to know:
S E R C O N	to be with

The word works parabolically, and its work, above all,
reworks the wordworker.

PALABRA ES PALA Y ABRA	Word is a shovel, an opening
PARA QUE ENTRE LA LUZ	for light to come in

The word is articulated silence and sound, organized
light and shadow.

It crisscrosses and combines forms of energy, it lets
sound see, the image hear.

Air or modulated breath, it simultaneously constructs
and destructs.

The double nature, the essential ambiguity that is the
source of asking questions.

The word creates the being, or is created by it, in a
mystery of which we only have the keys to make it grow.

Comparar, to compare: to stand beside.

"Our concepts owe their existence to comparisons."

"Something is present to us. It stands steadily by itself and thus manifests itself. It is. For the Greeks, 'being' basically meant this standing presence."

"*Logos* means the word, discourse, and *legein* means to speak, as in dia-logue, mono-logue. But originally *logos* did not mean speech, discourse... *Lego, legein,* Latin *legere,* is the same as the German word *lesen:* to gather, to collect, read... which is: to put one thing with another, to bring together, in short, to gather."
MARTIN HEIDEGGER, *An Introduction to Metaphysics*

Fragment 1: "But while the *logos* remains always this, men remain uncomprehending, both before they have heard and just after they have heard. For everything becomes essent in accordance with this *logos*..."

Fragment 2: "Therefore it is necessary to follow it, i.e., to adhere to togetherness in the essent; but though the *logos* is this togetherness in the essent, the many live as though each had his own understanding (opinion)."

Fragment 34: "Those who do not bring together the permanent togetherness hear but resemble the deaf."
HERACLITUS

Metaphor, from the Greek
metaphora, from
metapherein, to carry or
transfer. *Meta:* beyond.
Pherein: to carry.
                    JOAN COROMINAS

The metaphor carries beyond, toward the most complex
and the most specific forms of comparison; to the
furthest, the limits of knowledge, to the essence, the
heart of being, to its reason for being.

    CON RAZÓN   heart with reason

An essence dependent on the parabola that tracks it and
cannot be named other than by analogy or suggestion.

The metaphor carries beyond for love.

It searches for, desires the union of name and named.

"In Nahuatl the artist is *tlayolteuanni,* he who sees with his heart."

ELIOT WEINBERGER, *Selected Poems of Octavio Paz*

"Heart, *yóllotl,* in Nahuatl, is derived etymologically from the root *oll-in,* 'movement,' which in its abstract form *yóll-otl* signifies the idea of 'mobility,' the mobility of each one."

" ... in describing the supreme ideal of Nahua men and women, they say that they must be 'owners of a face, owners of a heart.' ... the supreme ideal of education, *Ixtlamachiliztli,* is the 'action of giving wisdom to the faces,' ... and *Yolmelahualiztli,* 'the action of straightening the heart.'"

MIGUEL LEÓN PORTILLA, *The Ancient Mexicans*

In the Popol Vuh (Maya Quiché) "God" is the "Heart of Heaven."

"Anything which moves, is moved because of something which it does not have, which thereby constitutes the end of its motion."

DANTE ALIGHIERI, *The Letter to Can Grande*

In the Hindu poetics, "a poem is recognized as such by 'those who have a heart.'"

RENÉ DAUMAL

"Who impels us to utter these words?
What cannot be spoken with words,
but that whereby words are spoken."
Kena Upanishad

One metaphor carries another within it; only poetry can
guarantee the continuance of the species.

A rising toward the precision where the metaphor
reaches terrains of splendor.

Splendor *is* creation.

A union of disparate forces, the word condenses
creation within its inner metaphors.

"According to Bhartrihari, two kinds of language exist. One is made from word-seeds *(sphota)*, ideas inalterables, that are modulations of the universal *atman*, the real divisions of the universe. (*Sphota* evokes the blossoming of a flower, the development of a bud – thus a constant germinative power hidden beneath the appearances which manifest it.) The other kind is created from sonorous words *(dhvani)*, usual words, subordinated to natural laws, that is to the rules of phonetics and grammar."

RENÉ DAUMAL, *Rasa*

"Sacred knowledge and, by extension, wisdom are conceived as the fruit of an initiation, and it is significant that obstetric symbolism is found connected with the awakening of consciousness both in ancient India and Greece. Socrates had good reason to compare himself to a midwife, for in fact he helped men to be born to consciousness of the self...The Buddha,...'engendered' by his 'mouth,' that is, by imparting his doctrine *(dharma)*."

MIRCEA ELIADE, *The Sacred and the Profane*

The Indo-European root *bher,* to carry, also, to bear children. Latin *ferre,* to carry, confer, differ, fertile, suffer; Greek *pherein,* to carry, amphora, euphoria, metaphor.

And *nomn-bher,* "to bear a name."

Poetry condenses the desire of words to create through union and multiplication.

The work of metaphor-making.

Words have a love for each other, a desire that culminates in poetry,

Union of man and his word, word with word.

For love we make words, not for necessity – for love is the only necessity.

VER DAD	truth:
DAR VER	to give sight
VERDADERA	truthful:
ES DADORA DE VER	giver of sight
VER EL SENTIDO DEL DAR	to see the meaning of giving
ES EL TRABAJO DEL	is the work of words
PALABRAR	

The word's desire to be, to grow and spread seems to be part of its being, as being means appearing, and desire means to shine.

Desire, from the Latin *desiderare*, to long for, formed in analogy with *considerare*, "to observe the stars carefully." *Sidus*, star, constellation: sidereal, from the Indo-European root *sweid*: to shine.

"... the word for 'god,' *deiw-os*, and the two-word name of the chief deity of the pantheon, *dyeu-pater* (Latin *Jupiter*, Greek *Zeus*, Sanskrit *Dyaus pitar*...) [are] derivatives of a root *deiw*, meaning to 'shine.'"

CALVERT WATKINS

"The nature of poetry, in turn, is the founding of truth."

MARTIN HEIDEGGER, Poetry, Language, Thought

"Truth, in Nahuatl, *neltiliztli*, is a term derived from the same root as *tla-nélhuatl*, which in turn is directly derived from *nelhuáyotl*, foundation."

"... etymologically, *truth* for the Nahuas was in its abstract form (*neltiliztli*), the quality of standing firmly, of being well grounded, of having good foundations."

MIGUEL LEÓN PORTILLA

Truth, in English, is derived from the Indo-European root *deru*, to be firm, solid, steadfast. Suffixed form variant *drew-o*, in Germanic *trewan*, in Old English *treow*, tree.

The word is the point of confluence and union, the ray in prayer.

A minimal, an essential poem, the word *is* poetry; to speak is to pray.

> *Flower is the word flower.*
> JOÃO CABRAL DE MELO NETO

The word has been created by and for poetry, and with poetry we give thanks for the grace we have received, life.

Oración in Spanish is speech and prayer at the same time. From the Latin *orare,* to speak and pray.

"Prayer is perfect when he who prays remembers not that he is praying."

ANONYMOUS

"What then did the voice of the first speaker say? I have no hesitation in saying that it must at once be clear to any man of sound mind that it was the word for 'God,' that is *El,* either as a question or as an answer."

DANTE ALIGHIERI, *De vulgari eloquentia*

"Thus in all poetry a word is like a sun."

ERNEST FENOLLOSA

"Poetry is a word whose essence is savor." (Sahitya Darpana) "'Savor' (*rasa*) is knowledge, 'shining in itself.'"

RENÉ DAUMAL

In the Mbyá Guaraní creation myth, love, language and
sacred song are created all at once:

> Appearing [in human form]
> from the wisdom inside his own light
> and by virtue of this creator wisdom
> he conceived the origin of human language
>
> Having conceived the origin of the future
> human language
> from the wisdom inside his own light
> and by virtue of this creator wisdom
> he conceived the idea of love [in union with the
> other]
>
> Having created the idea of human language
> having created a small sliver of love
> from the wisdom inside his own light
> and by virtue of this creator or wisdom
> he created in his loneliness
> the seed of a single sacred song
>
> And then
> from the wisdom inside his own light
> and by virtue of this creator wisdom
> he imparted
> to the true father of the future Karai
> to the true father of the future Tupa
> knowledge of this light
> To make true fathers of the word-souls
> of their many future children
> he imparted knowledge of this light
>
> *La Literatura de los Guaraníes*, LEÓN CADOGÁN,
> translated from the Spanish by DAVID GUSS

"There was nothing standing; only the calm water, the placid sea, alone and tranquil. Nothing existed.

"There was only immobility and silence in the darkness, in the night. Only the Creator, the Maker, Tepeu, Gucumatz, the Forefathers, were in the water surrounded with light. They were hidden under green and blue feathers, and were therefore called Quetzal Serpent. By nature they were great sages and great thinkers. In this manner the sky existed and also the Heart of Heaven, which is the name of God and thus He is called."

> So then came his word here.
>   It reached
> To Majesty
>   and Quetzal Serpent
> There in the obscurity,
>   In the nighttime.
> It spoke to Majesty
>   And Quetzal Serpent, and they spoke.
> Then they thought;
>   Then they pondered.
> Then they found themselves;
>   They assembled
> Their words,
>   Their thoughts.
> Then they gave birth –
>   Then they heartened themselves.

The Popol Vuh,
translated by MUNRO EDMONSON

"OM. This eternal Word is all: what was, what is and what shall be, and what beyond is in eternity. All is OM."

Mandukya Upanishad, translated by J U A N M A S C A R Ó

"In the beginning was the Word, and the Word was with God; and the Word was God."

S A I N T J O H N

" . . . by the fire of fervor arose the ONE. And in the ONE arose love. Love the first seed of the soul."

Rig Veda X,129

"Language falls, comes from above as little luminous objects that fall from heaven, which I catch word after word with my hands."

M A R Í A S A B I N A

"The word sign is radical supposedly from combination of tongue and above: ?"

E R N E S T F E N O L L O S A

"O fellow poets, we must take it upon ourselves
To stand, heads bared, beneath the tempests
Of the Lord, and seize the Father's lightning
With our hands, and offer the people
This gift of heaven, veiled in song."

FRIEDRICH HÖLDERLIN,
translated by Richard Sieburth

The common ground shared by these and so many other texts – what does it say? That we are all thinking together, but expressing ourselves in thousands of ways that are both different and the same? Or that an ancient wisdom, suppressed and forgotten, is revived in the poetic thought of every era?

To approach the one verse, the word as a uni-verse, is a uni-versal phenomenon.

To communicate is to listen.

COMUN UNICA ACCIÓN   communication:
                           common action

Communication contains the potential for common action.

What doors would listening together open?

From time immemorial, the word has wanted to speak. From the text *In the beginning was the Word . . .* and from our having been *created in His image and likeness* we could have learned that we are words, and all that is required of us is that we incarnate them, fully.

If the word creates, perhaps it is our creative nature that was being emphasized – and what have we created?

Universe, from the Indo-European root *wer*, to turn, from which Germanic *werth*, Old English *weard*, toward, inward, and *weorth*, worth, valuable...and the Latin *vertere*, to turn, *versare*, verse, version, universe.

The ancient Mesoamerican metaphor of "hearing the blood" is still alive in the shamanic practices, where "blood" is the location of the spirit, and thus it is "an animate substance, capable, in some individuals, of sending signals or speaking."

"...the blood passes from the heart and 'talks' at the joints, revealing the conditions and needs of the 'heart,' the curer only need 'listen to what the blood wants.'"

BARBARA TEDLOCK, *Time and the Highland Maya*

A wor(l)d that does not honor creation, that does not hear the working of words, nor distinguish between truth and lies?

Truth becomes a lie and lies truth.

But to see destruction brings another side to sight.

Being part of the truth, a lie can only increase it.

Hate is forked love say the Guaraní.

MENTIRA   lies:
TIRA O ROMPE LA MENTE   tear the mind apart

"You are aware that speech signifies all things and is always turning them round and round, and has two forms, true and false?"

"All things are in motion and progress and flux..."

PLATO, *Cratylus*

Language loses and gains its worth from earlier times.

Christ said: *What comes out of the mouth poisons man, not what goes into it.*

For Fenollosa, the anemia of modern speech arises from the feeble cohesive force of our phonetic symbols that no longer obviously display the metaphors that gave them birth.

For Socrates, the most imperfect state of a language is one that does not use appropriate likenesses.

For Heidegger, we do not see in language because we do not see in being, and it is the destruction of the relation to being that has impoverished the relation to language.

But that negation can only increase our desire: the use and the abuse of words that have obscured their reasons for being will ultimately illuminate words themselves:

"Our ancestors built the accumulations of metaphor into structures of language and into systems of thought. Languages today are thin and cold because we think less and less into them . . . Only scholars and poets feel painfully back along the thread of our etymologies and piece together our diction, as best they may, from forgotten fragments. This anemia of modern speech is only too well encouraged by the feeble cohesive force of our phonetic symbols . . . It does not bear its metaphor on its face. We forget that personality once meant, not the soul, but the soul's mask."

ERNEST FENOLLOSA, *The Chinese Written Character as a Medium for Poetry*

" . . . language in general is worn out and used up – an indispensable but masterless means of communication that may be used as one pleases, as indifferent as a means of public transport, . . . which everyone rides in . . . without hindrance and above all *without danger*.

"Man becomes human material, which is disposed of with a view to proposed goals." . . . "Modern Science and the total state, as necessary consequences of the nature of technology, are also its attendants. . . . Not only are living things technically objectivated in stock-breeding and exploitation; the attack of atomic physics on the phenomena of living matter as such is in full swing." . . . "What has long been threatening man with death, . . . is the unconditional character of mere willing in the sense of purposeful self-assertion in everything." . . . "The view that technological production puts the world in order, while in fact this ordering is precisely what levels every *ordo*, every rank, down to the uniformity of production, and thus from the outset destroys the realm from which any rank and recognition could arise.

"The self-assertion of technological objectivation is the constant negation of death. By this negation death itself becomes something negative."

MARTIN HEIDEGGER, *What Are Poets For*

When we speak, life speaks
Kaushitaki Upanishad

Wisdom is language
MARÍA SABINA

Sooner or later we will reach the consciousness of word-working, the shared knowledge that until now injustice and exploitation have impeded.

ASUMIR COLECTIVAMENTE to assume collectively
ELEGIR JUNTOS EL SER   to choose together   being

In *consciousness*, we unite two roots, *kom*, with, and *scire*, to know.

Kom, beside, near, by, with. Germanic *ga*, Old English *ge*, together. Latin *cum*, *co*, with. Suffixed form *kom-tra*, in Latin *contra*, against, suffixed form *kom-yo*, in Greek *koinos*, common, shared.

Sek, to cut, split, Latin *scire*, to know, "to separate one thing from another." Old English *scrim*, shin, shinbone, "piece cut off." Suffixed form *skiy-ena*, Old Irish *scian*, knife, Germanic *skitan*, to separate, defecate. Suffixed form *sk(h)id-yo*, in Greek *skhizein*, split.

Demo (the root for democracy), comes from the root *da, dai*, to divide. Suffixed form *da-mo*, division of society, *demos*, people, land. (Those who divide among themselves what there is.)

Universe says: verse becomes one only in the union of every one, and of everyone and God.

Light, love, and language are formed simultaneously in the creation myth.

The word says: only by being one does the way *to those who redeem speech* open for us, giving back to the word the power to speak to us.

Every form has a force.

The force that finds its own vibration.

The word is the breath of love armed to inspire love for the great poem: creation.

"Think of the constellations, they too are forms."

PIET MONDRIAN

"All truth has to be expressed in sentences because all truth is the transference of power."

ERNEST FENOLLOSA

"'Is' comes from the Aryan root *as*, to breathe."

ERNEST FENOLLOSA

"The breath of life is one."

KAUSHITAKI UPANISHAD

III

La Wik'uña

La luz es el primer animal visible de lo invisible.

Light is the first visible animal of the invisible.

JOSÉ LEZAMA LIMA

Iridesce

¿Adónde van
los suaves innúmeros

Apiñándose en haz?

La luz
los desea

Y los sale
a buscar

Pétalo
y pluma

Concha
y piedrá

Piel de semilla
petróleo en el mar

Brusco lo brusco

Huequito ancestral

Supina membrana

Cilia
natal

Rayos radiando

Lúcido entrar

Iridesce

Where do they go
all those soft rays

gathering in a knot?

Light desires
& seeks them

Petal
& feather

Shell
& stone

The seed's skin
shines oily in the sea

Brusque
brisk

Ancestral little hollow

Supine membrace

Native
cilia

Rays flashing

Blinding entrance

El mismo brillo
sabe pensar

Todo es
sombrita

Cambiante
irisar

Nupcian
quebrando

Su lomo
lustral

Relumbra
huachito!

Ojo pulsar

Entrevera
tu alianza

Poro prismal

Ofrenda
es el iris

Arco visual

Oscura
la fuente

Negro
el brillar

The same radiance
thinks

Tiny shadow
they are

Turning iridescence

A lustrous
back flips

Shine again
little waif!

You,
throbbing eye

glimpse
an ally

Prismal pore

Offering
the iris

Visual
bow

Dark is
the fountain

Shining
black!

[S J L]

Light is sacred as it enters all kinds of prisms, the pores of the skin, feathers or seashells.

Reflections are prayers of light.

Iris, from the Greek *to turn,* is both the eye and the messenger.

Jechaka mba' ekuaa (Guaraní), reflection of his wisdom, thought of the creator, organ of sight, birth of the sun.

The message is light.

The iridescent hummingbird is the messenger.

¿Tienes algo que comunicar, Colibrí?
¡Lanza rayos el Colibrí!
– El jugo de tus flores evidentemente
te ha mareado, Colibri.
¡Lanza rayos, lanza rayos, Colibri!

Canto del Colibrí
(Chiripá Guaraní)

Have something to say, Hummingbird?
Hummingbird flashes rays of light
The juice from your flowers
has made you dizzy
Hummingbird flashes
rays of light!

Song of the Hummingbird
(Chiripá Guaraní)

[S J L]

Tentenelaire Zun Zun

La luz
en ti
goza

Traga néctar
lumbrón

Espejo
que vuela

Oro tornasol

Cáliz corola
bicho fulgor

Vence
a la muerte

Altarcito
licor

Niño lenguando

Chupá
picaflor!

Nadie es
lo frágil

Lo pálpita
fuerte

Zit Zit, Hummingbird

Light
plays
upon you

sip nectar
bird-fly

Mirror
in flight

Iridescent gold

Chalice of petals
shining critter

beat death
nectarine

liquor
shrine

Child licking

Sip sip
hummingbird

Nobody
so fragile

Quicker than quick
heartbeats

Pico
en perfume

Prismá
volador

Limina
tu lumen

Ven a trabajar

Viso
y derrumbe

Cálamo
zúm

Sueña
zumbando

¡No pares
aún!

Beak
in perfume

Flying
prism

light of the edge

I'm off to work

Gleam
and crumble

Humming
          feather

Dream
whirring

don't stop!

[S J L]

El poema
es el animal

Hundiendo la boca

En el manantial

The poem is the animal

Sinking its mouth
in the stream

La Wik'uña

La wik'uña
es pastar y correr

Pecho blanco
al atardecer

Cúspido brote
a todo dar

Cerril corpar

Ojos colmando
el cabezal

Flor del lanio
y del ultra fugaz

Me duermo
en tu potestad

Perder la cabeza
y volverla a recuperar

Lo wikuño
del wikuñar

Pensar lumínico
y cabal

Fase de hilo

Wik'uña

Wik'uña being
is grazing & running

White breast
at nightfall

Sprout on a peak
exploding

Wilderness in one body

Eyes overflowing
its little head

Wooly flower
slipping by

I sleep
in your domain

Lose my head
go back to find it

Wik'uñanessence
of wik'uñaty

Thought
as perfect light

Filament

Entrando
en el cristal

Fibra de orar

Poliedro impensable

Y ahí está

Tú que comes
y ludes

Tú que eres
y eludes

Fina devolvedora
del sentido

La fuerza
entre nos

Amanecer
del amar siendo
el animal

Pálpita pálpita
saltarina

Señora de las
altitudes andinas

Tú eres mi
cósica calórica
camótica

Piercing crystal

Fiber of prayer

Geometry
unexpected

& suddenly there

You who eats
& scrapes

You who are
escapes

Restorer
of meanings

Strength
between us

Animal
rising
from our love

Our Lady of the Andes
leap

You're my
tomato
my chili pepper
hot potato

Mi cáspita bruces

La Cupisnique

Tú eres la Uru
y la Bamba

Qué andas haciendo

Apu aquí
oro en monte
Rimac allá

Qué andas haciendo

Wik'uña al monte
tres prístinos mugidos
tres rápidos tris-trás

Salvaje y frugal

Vivísima fuente
del lanar

Pelo al sol

Hija y madre
del tiempo mejor

Aquí te vas
y tu ijar se vuelve
grupa tonaz

Tú lo has querido
mandado y dolido

¿A qué te soy?

My whoops
clunk

You're the Cupisnique

Uru
and Bamba

What are you doing

The Apu here
gold on the mountain
and the Rimac there

What are you doing

Wik'uña on the mountain
three snorts
three sharps she's off

Wild and frugal

Effervescent
fountain of wool

Rug in the sun

Mother and daughter
of better times

You're off
and your legs
are thunder

You wanted
demanded it suffered

Why am I you?

Wikuñar y pastar

Mover el pelo
al norte y al sur

¿A qué flaquita?

Pepita de ají

¿A qué has venido?

Be Wik'uña and graze

Take your rug
north and south

Hey skinny
for what?

Pepper pot

Why have you come?

Thread of water, thread of life, people say the wik'uñas
are born where the springs are born.

Fiber of prayer, to weave is to pray.

Spun gold, riches and fertility.

"The earth receives love when it is offered food and
drink wrapped in cloth made from wik'uña, for the
wik'uña is the animal of the earth."

BERNABE CONDORI and ROSALIND GOW

Aguará

a C . P .

Zorrito de piel eterna
Aguará

Tú eres mi casa
y cintura

Mandra raposa

Chilla añás

Trayendo
andas visiones

Y en la cola
te revolotean aviones

Mosca a la miel
color al pincel

Golpe
al claro

Brillo
al oscuro

Manda el contorno
vive el compás

Ojo umbral
verde vitral

Salta el salmón
cobalto chillón

Zorro de ver

Fox

for C . P.

Little fox
your fur forever

My house
and waist

Crazy like a
sly cunning outfoxed
foxy lady

Carrying visions
never fail

Airplanes circle
around your tail

Fly to honey
color to the brush

Whack
at light

Alight
at dark

The edge rules
the line beats

Doorway eye:
beach glass green

Salmon leap
shriek of blue

Seeing-eye fox

Wari y Nazca
vuelve a comer

Entra al templo
pórfido quarz

Ollanta y tambo
la entraña más

Germina la puerta

Poroto cuadrado
de sacro ser

Lento el zarpe

Olisquea la huella

Del templo
a la tela

Pinturea la cola
y quién alcanza

La zorra entereza
de tu cabeza

Deslumbra entrepierna

Curva recién
nacida

Visión vuelta
a la vida.

Feeding
Wari & Nazca

Entering the temple
Porphyry quartz

Ollanta & tambo
more than the buried guts

The door sprouts

Squared bean
of sacred being

Paw slowly raised

Sniffing the track

From the temple
to the canvas

Your tail painting
what can compare

Your head
never cornered

Lights up
the inner thigh

Curve
newly born

vision given
life

[S J L / E W]

"There are always foxes where there are wik'uñas. The foxes hunt and eat the wik'uña babies. The wik'uñas defend their young . . . attacking the fox in groups, kicking it until it falls . . . the cries of the hapless fox are useless, for in the end it succumbs to the hooves of the wik'uñas."

BERNABE COBO

Las oraciones son los hilos y el tejido es la aparicion de la luz.

Prayers are threads and weaving is the birth of light.

JOSÉ LEZAMA LIMA

Oro es tu hilar

Oro
es tu hilo
de orar

Templo
del siempre
enhebrar

Armando casa
del mismo
treznal

Teja mijita
no más

Truenos y rayos
bordando al pasar

Tuerce
que tuerce

El dorado
enderezo

El fresco
ofrendar

Ñustas calmadas
de inquieto pensar

Marcas señales

Pallá y pacá

Gold Is Your Spinning

Gold
is your thread
of prayer

Temple
of forever
threading eyelet

Your house built
from the same
braid

Weave on

Thunder & lightning
embroidered as you go

Twisting
and twisting

Till the gold
rises

A fresh
offering

The unquiet thoughts
of the quiet weaving girl

Marks & signs

Here & there

Hilos y cuerdas

Los negros
y los dorá

Cavilan
el punto

No se vaya
a escapar

Hilo y vano

Lleno y vacío

El mundo
es hilván

Pierdo
el hilo

Y te hilacho
briznar

Código y cuenta
cómputo comunal

Todo amarran

Hilando
en pos

Cuerdas y arroyos

The threads & strings

Black
& gold

Thinking
before each stitch

Not to let it drop

A grid
of empty space

A fabric of holes

The world
is a loose stitch

I've lost
the thread

but I rag on

It's a code
and a count

an account
of the people

Tying it all

Threading
towards it all

Aunar lo tejido

¿No es algo
inicial?

El cálido fuelle

Oro templar

Habla y abriga

El mejor juglar

Streams & strings

The stars
the river weaves

The woven
woven into one

A thing of origin

Hot bellows

Tempered gold

A troubador's
words & cape

[S J L / E W]

Quechua, the sacred language, is conceived as a thread.

"Quechua possibly derives from *q'eswa:* a rope made of twisted reeds."

JORGE LIRA

"Mysteries are revealed by putting it all together."

ROBERT RANDALL

Watuq, the shaman, is "he who ties," from *watuy,* to tie.
Watunasimi, the woven language, creates the world through oracles, parables and prophecies.
Hatunsimi, the principal language, uses archaic words with many meanings, palindromes, and borrowings from other languages.
Chantaysimi, beautiful speech, is embroidered speech.

But they did not write, they wove.

" . . . there was a sacred writing, a type of hieroglyphic system composed of symbols ordered or combined together, which finds its richest expression in weaving."

UBBELOHDE-DOERING

Weaving is union.

Hanan/Hurin, high and low, full and empty, man and woman.

Una
es el agua
y su misma
sed

Water
and its thirst
are one

Unuy Quita

Undísono magma
curvó manantial

Pacha pacarina
esfera y turbión

Una sola eres

Aguaá

Meandro
tu kenko

Gozo espiral

¿Quién te ensució?

Chichita
challando

Splasha jugando

Tu bolsa
y mi nado

Una sola sed!

Unuy Quita

Curving soundulating
magmatic stream

Pacha Pacarina
flashflood sphere

You are one

Waterrrr

Zigzag meander

Spiraling joy

Who filled you with filth?

Chicha gone
around the bend

Playing splashing

Your sack
my span

One thirst!

¡Estremezca sed!

Azapa fecunda

Parina redonda

Sacra cohera

Mismándose!

Fluye
tu siempre

Anda
en tu sangre

Fluyéndose

Taza
en neblina

Tu mismo
ser

Shiver you thirst!

Fertile valley

Round waterbird

Sacred you cohere

Being yourself!

Flow
forever

Travel
through your blood

Flowing
through yourself

Cup
in the mist

You
yourself

The Earth, a drop of water in the void.

Sacrificial amniotic fluid, communion vessel.

To contaminate a stream is to contaminate all of them.

Sewage and watershed sooner or later will find each
other.

Clean singing, sprinkling with holy water.

Mother of the water, zigzag serpent.

*

Love in its most ancient form is *luba,* thirst.

Phuyumama licenciakimanta

Madre de las nubes licencia pido
para pasar

Mother of clouds grant me leave
to go through

HIGHLAND PRAYER

¡Neblinilla fibrosa!
Neblinilla ciempiés

Fragando frugando
su fertilidad

¡Cuiden sus llamas!
¡Cuiden su lisor!

¡Qué hermoso
qué hermoso!

Dijo y despertó

Así lo traía
de vuelta en visor

Así lo subía
brillando en su haz

¡Fueguito sagrado!

¡Ofrendilla de mies!

Foggy little fog

Fibrous little fog!
Foggy centipede

Scenting
fertility dancing

We must take care of her flames!
Take care of her smoothness!

How beautiful!
How bountiful!

She said and awoke

Thus she brought all this
back in view

Thus she raised it
shining in its crisscross

Sacred little fire!

Offering of grain

[S J L]

Se acabará
la fuente redonda
la propia silencia
la sílbida clave

¡Se acabará!

¿Dónde se irá la neblina?
¿La bruma vivificante?
¿Dónde se irá?

Fresco, fresco

¡El sostén de la tierra!
¡Los racimos de llanto!

¡Los corazones apagados
sin neblinar!

The round spring
its own silence
the sylvan key
will end

It will all end!

Where will the fog go?
The life-giving mist?
Where will it go?

Cool, fresh,

The earth's sustenance
The tear-filled branches

Our hearts extinguished
when the fog is gone!

[SJL]

Mist is the semen of the mountains
where the streams are born

Mist is the semen of the forest
where coolness is born

The Guaraní of the rain forest in Paraguay and Brazil say
that when the mist and the forest are gone, we will all be
gone.

Offering burnt by the Inka,
cloth returns to eternity

Humar

Tenue
es mi traje

Hilo y dulzor

Aire voluto

Trino
en formón

Canto
en despliego

Y en humo
me voy

Otila vibrante
y rozna al bajar

Hollínate
capno

Ven a trabajar!

Humoso fecundo
ponte pallá

Espira curvo
y ven a torcer

Smoke

My tenuous
dress

Thread & sugar

Spiraling air

Chiselled trill

Song
uncurving

I go up in smoke

Oteeela vibrating
hissing as it comes down

Soot
yourself

Get to work!

Smoky lush
go to it

Spin curve
come braid

Vólvido
vuelve

A tu mismo
vual!

Whirlwind
back

To your
veils

[S J L / E W]

"I'm a smoke paper woman."
                              MARÍA SABINA

                Language of wood
                incense and copal
                food of thread
                spiral ascent

"Like the human ear, the spiral encloses the primordial
sound."
                              RENÉ GUÉNON

Ollantaytambo

Ollanta, Ollanta
¿dónde viste la voz?

El hondo sílabo
cruzando el río

El cuerpo
y la entraña

Del Aguador?

Abismo
a pico

Perfume
en calor?

Ahí, ahí
en el templo
guardián

Roca
que enciende
el amanecer

Rosa cúbico
vertical

Tetas brotando
del puro piedrar

Ollantaytambo

Ollanta, Ollanta
where did you see the voice?

The deep syllabia
crossing the river

The body
& the guts

Of the Water Man?

Steep
Abyss

Perfume
heat rising

There, there
in the guardian
temple

Rock lit
by dawn

Vertical
cubic rose

Tits bursting
out of pure stone

Pórfido
trapezoidal

Dolobre
canteado

Y arista
pelá

Saliente
labrada

Vertiente
en canal

¿Quién te abandonó?

Lasca y acequia
cuña y baivel?

Riego y gozo
a la vez?

¡Solas
las piedras

El pórfido
quarz

Peldaños
y ofrendas

Sin trabajar!

Porphyry
trapezoid

Hammered
border

Bare
edge

Wrought
ledge

Stream
channeled

Who abandoned you?

Chip & gutter
bevel & wedge?

You spray & enjoy
at once?

Alone
the stones

Porphyry
quartz

Steps
& offerings

Don't work!

Agüita
que enjuga
su aguar

Tú la hiciste
sagrada

Bajando
a regar

Altar abierto

Sonar

Murmullo
de cantizal

Arar y orar

¡Todo junto
Aymoray!

Little water
becoming
itself

You made it
sacred

Coming down
to spray

Open altar

Sounding

Stony ground
murmur

Plow & pray

All together
Aymoray!

[S J L]

Inkamisana

Escaleras y ritos
no para el pie

Edificio
que piensa

Roca angular

Verde rascacielos

Negro zigurat

Miniatura
de tiempo

Trocado
en altar

Invento
de noche

Saliente
al albar

Roca tallada
en brotes
de orar

Búsquido rasgo
de lo germinal!

Saliva
en torrente

Inkamisana

Stairs & rites
not for the foot

The building
thinks

Angular rock

Green skyscraper

Black ziggurat

Miniature
of time

Made
into altar

Invention
of the night

Sprouting
at dawn

Carved rock
praying
as it buds

Seeking the seed
to sprout!

Saliva
in torrents

Arrullo
de aguar

Redime tu cancha

Cabeza de sal

Arroyo
de luces

Doble reflejar

La piedra
y el agua

El mismo
brotar

Cooling waterfall

You redeem your field

Salt head

Stream
of lights

Double reflection

Stone
& water

The same
sprouting

[SJL]

Broto

Broto
que mana

Cogollo
simplón

Cargo
potente

Salado
torpor

Raijo
es tu bulto

Espeso
fulgor

Retoña
y arraiga

Negracho
botón

Macolla
y pulula

Ardido
calor

Brótalo
pronto

Bud

Bud
a flood

Hard
core

Charged
force

Drowsy
salt-lick

Your swelling
a sprouting

Thick
splendor

Shoot
take root

Silk-black
blossoms

Cluster
& swarm

Fever
heat

Soon
springs

Quéspero
yo

Brótalo
dando

Qués solo
tirón

I

wait you

Bursting
springing

You, sprout
sprung

> "I am a sprouting woman."
>
> MARÍA SABINA

Seedbed of images in the sun.

Hokyani (Quechua): to sprout, to burst, to blossom.
Simicta hokyachicuni: to discover a secret, to inadvertently
reveal: "to spill the beans."

Yacha: to know.
Yachacuni: to grow, as in a seedbed.

Amtaña (Aymara): to remember
Amutatha, amu: the bud of a flower.

"to walk empty" is not to remember,
to have no "flower inside."

Selvaje Matar

Descuajo y resalvo
venturo mental

Raja sueño
de lo lento
y neutral

Empecina
y alienta

Ramita real

Arracima
y redoma

Manojo apical

Valva pubescente

Entrando
a jugar

Te humo
y alabo

Hacho
y menoscabo

Selvaje
matar

Bulldoza
tu sierra

Jungle Kill

I uproot & save
mental venture

I split the dream
of the slow
& neutral

Persist
& breathe

My little flask

Pointy wisp

Pubescent valve

Join
the game

I smoke
& praise you

Hew
& raze you

Jungle
kill

Bulldoze
your sierra

Fuego
y cenizal

Yo espera
y espera

Y tú
dónde vas

Perfume
y lantana

Acierta
tu voz

En llanos
calmados

Y silencio
feroz

Borrar
lo sediento

Ingrávido
altar

Insulto
a la sangre

Alertá
diagonal

¡Pudre
y aguanta!

Fire
to ash

I wait
& wait

And you
where are you

Fragrant
lantana

Aim
your voice

In calm
plains

In silence
wild

Erasing
the thirst

The weightless
altar

insults
the blood

Awake
diagonals

Rot
& Stand

Va y va

Flora
en ganancia

Plantá voluntá!

Go & go

Flower
gaining

Plant your will!

[S J L]

The strength of the jungle receding!

Botanical splendor, the flooded world!

"So, you will watch over the fountain of mist where inspired words are born..."

MBYA GUARANÍ

Rain and mist are the laws of fertility and moderation.

"Only this: those who are destined to gather and rise on this earthly abode will live in harmony, though they may wish to wander from the love that brings them together."

MBYA GUARANÍ

Guainambí Tominejo El Ultimo Colibrí

Guainambí
tominejo

El último
colibrí

Alentando
su cuero

Antes
de dormir

Chinchorros
perpetuos

Alisos
de lleno

Con tanto
silencio

Y tantísimo
aliento

¡Vengan mis chirridos!

De frente
y de rayo

Bruscando
perfil

Guainambí Tominejo, The Last Hummingbird

Guainambí
Tominejo

The last
hummingbird

Bracing
his skin

Before going
to sleep

Perpetual
swarms

Sleek
full of
wind

So
silent

Breathing so

Come squeak and streak

Straight
beaming rays

Sudden turn

¡Aquí todo es bacano!
¡Aquí todo es obeso!

Sombrita
de fieltro

Matando
pulmón

¡Esmoga tu llama
mi picaflor!

Desecho
rubiando

En el basural

Bailando
un reflejo

¡Todos
se irán!

Here all is sweet!
Here all are obese!

Dusky
felt shadow

Panting
to death

Smogged in flames
my hummingbird!

Broken
Blonding

In the
wasteland

a reflection
dancing

All
will go away!

[S J L]

In Quito I saw hummingbirds that followed the traffic lights like a truck. They turned the corners searching for flowers on the balconies.

In Santiago I saw them in their mating dance over the garbage dump in Conchalí: the males in zigzag flight flashing red to attract the best female.

Ba Surame

Bá
surame

Sura
en mí

Ven a
surear

Séme
Sur

Sur ame
ya!

Litter Me

A little
litter

Lit in me

Alit on me
alive in me

A litter love

Alit

If you open the word *Basurame* (turn me into garbage),
it becomes a command: love the south.

Glossary

A P U R I M A C (Quechua). *Apu,* lord. *Rimac,* speaker, "the lord who speaks." A river that unites with the Urubamba to form the Ucayali. There was an oracle on its banks.

A Y M O R A Y (Quechua). Harvest festival.

C H A L L A R (Hispanized Quechua). To sprinkle, to spray, to offer.

C U P I S N I Q U E. A ravine south of the river Jequetepe, on the north coast of Peru, site of the culture of the same name, circa 1200 B.C., noted for its ceramic sculpture.

H A N A N / H U R I N (Quechua). High and low. Complementary halves of the Andean communities, which were divided into two sectors.

H U A C H O. "Young man" in the Mochica language, it came to mean an orphan or an indigent in Quechua. In the popular speech of Chile, Peru and Argentina, it means, interchangeably, a natural son, an illegitimate son, and an orphan.

I N K A M I S A N A. "The message of the Inka." A mixed Quechua and Spanish word, derived from *inka* or *enka,* the life force or vital principle, and *misa,* from the Latin *missa est,* from *mittere,* to send, a missive, a mission. Part of the ceremonial center of Ollantaytambo.

I R I S. From the proto-Indo-European *wei,* to fold or bend. In grade zero form, *wi-ri,* from which derives the Greek *iris,* Spanish *arcoiris,* the rainbow and the goddess of the rainbow, messenger of the gods.

K E N K O (Quechua). Zigzag.

K' IJLLU. "This word in Quechua means the cracks in the rocks. Not ordinary rocks, but the huge ones, the ones with endless veins that run irregularly across the mountain ranges, forming the foundations of the snow-capped peaks that blind the traveler with their brightness." (José María Arguedas).

NECTAR. From the Greek *nekrós*, death. Iris fed the gods with nectar. The hummingbird, symbol of resurrection, eats nectar.

OLLANTAYTAMBO. A town to the northeast of Cuzco, whose ceremonial center was under construction when the Spanish arrived. Designed by the Inka Pachakuti, who organized the flow of the waters into a complete system of irrigation canals, baths and shrines with the "express sentiment of purification," according to Luis Valcárcel.

PACARINA (Quechua). Place of origin.

PACHA (Quechua-Aymara). Earth, space-time.

PARINA (Aymara). Flamingo.

QUIPU (KHIPU) (Quechua). Knot, a spatial system of annotation for government statistics and poetic and musical composition in the Inka and pre-Inka periods. "It consisted of a series of cords of cotton or wool in codified colors, knotted at regular intervals, and attached in turn to a larger cord from which they hung."

UNUY QUITA (Quechua). "You my lovely waters." A song of four syllables, whose repeated sounds represent water falling on the rocks.

URUBAMBA. Branch of the Amazon, called *Willkamayu*, "sacred river" (Quechua). Along its banks are Ollantaytambo and Machu Picchu.

About the Author

Cecilia Vicuña was born in Santiago de Chile in 1948. After studying Fine Arts at the University of Chile, she went to London in 1972 on a British Council scholarship. The military coup of 1973 forced her to remain in England, where she was active in opposition movements, published her first bilingual book of poetry, exhibited at the Institute of Contemporary Arts, and was the subject of a BBC documentary (under an assumed name).

In 1975 she returned to South America. Based in Colombia, she traveled extensively throughout the continent, continuing her studies of Andean shamanism, oral traditions, mythology and herbal lore. In 1980, she moved to New York City, where she continues to live.

The author of seven books of poetry, she has performed "ritual readings" throughout the U.S., Europe and Latin America. Her films, installations and performance pieces have been exhibited at the Museum of Modern Art and the New Museum in New York, as well as at museums in Amberes, Berkeley, Bogotá and Santiago de Chile, among others.

The recipient of many honors, she received the Human Rights Award from the Fund for Free Expression in 1985, and was invited to the Bellagio Study Center in Italy in 1990. Her poetry was recently the subject of a one-hour documentary in the Rohm & Haas "Poet Vision" series.

About the Translators

Suzanne Jill Levine is a prolific translator of Latin American writing, including work by Manuel Puig, Carlos Fuentes, Adolfo Bioy Casares, José Donoso, Guillermo Cabrera Infante, Severo Sarduy and others. Her exploration of her art, *The Subversive Scribe: Translating Latin American Fiction*, was recently published by Graywolf.

Eliot Weinberger is the author of two collections of essays, *Works on Paper* and *Outside Stories*, both published by New Directions. Among his translations are the *Collected Poems of Octavio Paz 1957–1987*, Jorge Luis Borges's *Seven Nights*, and Vicente Huidobro's *Altazor*, which was published in Graywolf's *Palabra Sur* series.

Photo credits:

Con Cón by Ricardo Vicuña

Autumn by Carlos Baeza

A Glass of Milk by Oscar Monsalve

The Chibcha Trail by Oscar Monsalve

All others by César Paternosto

This book is set in Palatino type

by The Typeworks and manufactured by

Thomson-Shore, Inc.

on acid-free paper.